Bun wanted to earn some money for a new mackintosh, so he and Click went round with an ice-cream barrow.

A Red Fox Book
Published by Random House Children's Books
20 Vauxhall Bridge Road, London SW1V 2SA

A division of Random House UK Ltd

London Melbourne Sydney Auckland
Johannesburg and agencies throughout the world

1 3 5 7 9 10 8 6 4 2

First published in Great Britain by
George Newnes Limited 1946

Red Fox edition 1994

Set in Optima
by Intype, London

Printed and bound in Great Britain by
Cox & Wyman Ltd, Reading, Berkshire

RANDOM HOUSE UK Limited Reg. No. 954009
ISBN 0 09 928991 1

JOSIE, CLICK AND
BUN AGAIN

Enid Blyton

Illustrated by Dorothy M. Wheeler

RED FOX

Do you remember Josie, Click and Bun, who used to live in the little Tree-House?

You remember Josie was a big doll, Bun was a darling rabbit, and Click was a clockwork mouse.

Well, one day a dreadful thing happened. The woodmen came to mark all the trees that were to be cut down, and –

They marked the tree where Josie, Click and Bun lived! 'Oh, oh, what are we to do? Where shall we live?' cried Bun.

'We must leave our darling Tree-House and look for somewhere else to live,' said Josie. 'Come along – we will go and look now.'

So all three of them went house-hunting. They saw a fine house to let in a toadstool, but it was too small. Only Click could have got in at the door.

They saw a cave in the hillside with a nice front door, but Josie felt sure it would be very dark inside.

And then they saw just exactly the house they would like! It was made out of an old train carriage!

'Oh, look,' cried Bun. 'A house made of an old train carriage! What fun! It has a chimney – and doors – and windows.'

'And it is to let,' said Josie. 'Come along – let's get the key and go and look at it. I believe it would just suit us.'

They got the key and went to look at the train-house.
There was a bedroom, a sitting-room and a kitchen, all
exactly the same size.

'Let's live here,' said Click. 'I'd like to live in part of an
old train. Josie, do let's move here, please do!'

9

Well, it was all decided. The little Tree-House family were
to move into the old train carriage. Bun went to borrow
a big barrow.

'I can put our furniture in it,' he said. 'I shall have to make
a lot of journeys to and fro, but never mind.'

Josie packed everything neatly. Bun wheeled the furniture bit by bit to the new house. And then Click disappeared!

'Where's Click?' said Josie. 'I haven't seen him for a long time.' 'Nor have I,' said Bun. 'Click, where are you?' But no Click came.

Josie and Bun hunted everywhere for Click. They looked all round the Tree-House, and called him loudly. But he didn't come.

Then they went to the Train-House, and looked in all the rooms there. 'Click!' they called. 'Click!' And then they heard his little voice.

12

'I'm here! I'm here! Josie, I'm here!' But still they couldn't see him anywhere, though they looked under the beds and even inside the stove.

Then they found him! He had got into one of the drawers of the big chest, and Josie had shut him in without knowing! *Wasn't* he glad to be let out!

At last the little family were settled into their new home. They liked it very much. 'There are no stairs here as there were at the Tree-House,' said Josie.

'It will be fun to make new friends,' said Bun. 'Look, there goes Mrs. Trot-About, who lives in the old cottage nearby.'

14

Click Gets A Big Balloon!

'I like her. She sells lovely balloons,' said Click. 'Please can I have one, Josie? I want a blue one, a very big one.'

So Josie gave Click a penny and he ran after Mrs. Trot-About and her bunch of balloons. He bought the biggest she had!

The balloon was bigger than Click. He played with it for a time, letting it blow on the wind behind him. And then . . .

. . . A big gust came, and instead of Click pulling the balloon, the balloon pulled Click! Away he went over the fields!

Click Is Being Blown Away!

'Gracious!' said Josie. 'Look at Click! He's being blown away. Go after him, Bun, or he will be lost again.'

Click was blown ever so far. Somehow he didn't think of letting go the string. He bounced up and down as he went!

Suddenly the balloon blew into a holly bush. The prickles pricked it – and BANG, the balloon burst!

Click was dreadfully upset. He sat down and wept loudly. 'My balloon has gone pop! I'm lost, I'm lost! What shall I do?'

18

Home On The Bus!

But Bun was not far off. He had hurried after Click as fast as ever he could. He ran to him and comforted him.

'Look, there's a bus,' he said. 'It will take us home. That will be a treat. Don't cry any more, Click.' So Click dried his tears and they went home on the bus.

Josie, Click and Bun liked Mrs. Trot-About, the balloon-woman, and they liked Mister Pop the Brownie, who sold ginger-beer and ice-creams.

But they didn't like a queer old woman who lived in a most peculiar house. It was a very big Shoe.

20

'She's the Old Woman Who Lives in a Shoe,' said Josie.
'But now her children are grown up, and she lives alone.'

'She is a cross person,' said Bun. 'I would like to tease
her.' 'You'd better not,' said Josie. 'She might whip you and
put you to bed.'

Now Bun badly wanted to play a trick on the Old Woman Who Lived in a Shoe. So he did something very naughty indeed.

He and Click climbed all the way up the Shoe to the chimney at the top. And then Bun poured water down from a jug.

Bun Is Naughty!

The Old Woman was sitting in her funny room inside the Shoe and suddenly the fire went 'sizzle-sizzle-sizzle!'

'What's happening?' cried the Old Woman, and she went outside to see if the rain was pouring down the chimney. And she saw Bun and Click!

Well, the Old Woman caught Click and Bun, and she took them into her house. 'You bad creatures,' she cried.

'I shall keep you here to live with me, and teach you manners. I've no children now, so you will do instead.'

She made them sup some broth out of a cup. Bun spilt his and the Old Woman was cross with him.

Then she whipped them and put them into two little beds. They did cry. 'Josie! Josie!' wept Click. 'Please come and save us.

25

Josie waited and waited for Bun and Click to come home.
But they didn't. Mrs. Trot-About said she hadn't seen
them.

Nor had Mister Pop. 'I hope they haven't played a trick
on the Old Woman,' he said. 'She is sure to catch them
if they have.'

'I'll go and see,' said Josie. So out she went into the night, and soon came to the Shoe. She peeped in through a window, and saw . . .

. . . Bun and Click in their little beds, crying for her! The Old Woman was fast asleep in her chair.

Josie climbed in quietly through the window. She tiptoed to Bun and Click. They *were* glad to see her. 'Ssh!' said Josie. 'Ssh!'

Bun and Click got out of bed. Josie put their pillows down their bed under the clothes to make them look like Click and Bun.

Then Click went to climb out of the window. But he knocked over a fern-pot there, and down it went with a crash!

The Old Woman woke up at once. Josie, Click and Bun crouched down behind a big armchair. 'Now what was that noise?' said the Old Woman, and she got up.

The Old Woman looked at the two little beds to make sure that Click and Bun were still there. She saw the bumps made by the pillows.

'It couldn't have been Click and Bun making that noise,' she said. 'I must have dreamed it.' So she sat down again and fell asleep.

Then Bun, Click and Josie climbed quickly out of the window and ran home as fast as they could in the darkness.

Josie put Bun and Click to bed. 'You can tell me all that happened tomorrow,' she said, rather sternly. 'I think you must both have been rather naughty.'

Next morning Bun had to tell Josie the trick he and Click had played on the Old Woman. 'I am really ashamed of you,' said Josie.

'You must go and say you are sorry.' 'But the Old Woman will catch us again,' said Bun. 'I will go with you,' said Josie.

Bun And Click Are Sorry!

So, holding Bun and Click by the hand, she took them to the Old Woman. 'I'm very sorry I was naughty,' said Bun. 'So am I,' said Click.

'Well, I'll forgive you this time,' said the Old Woman. 'I can see that Josie is bringing you up nicely, so you will not need to be taught by me after all!'

One day Bun went out into the rain and got very wet.
'Dear, dear, you need a mackintosh,' said Josie. 'But I've
no money to buy you one.'

'I will earn some,' said Bun. 'Mr. Pop wants a boy to go
round with his ice-creams this week, because he isn't
well.'

34

So Bun went round with a hand-barrow on which were bottles of ginger-pop, and a tub of ice-cream. Click went with him.

Bun thought it was fun. He sold ginger-pop and ice-cream and then he and Click sat down and had some, too. It was all so nice that they had more and more!

Josie saw Click and Bun eating the ice-creams. 'How silly you are!' she said. 'The money you will have to pay for the ginger-beer and ice-cream will be more than Mr. Pop will give you for going round with them.'

So the next day Bun and Click didn't have any ginger-pop or ice-cream at all. They just ate the sandwiches Josie made for them.

At the end of the week Mr. Pop paid them. There was just enough money to buy a mackintosh for Bun!

He did look grand in his new mackintosh. It was a pretty blue, and had a sou'wester, too. Don't you think he looks nice in it?

Every day Bun wanted it to rain, because he had a new mackintosh. He was so disappointed because Josie wouldn't let him wear it.

'It's not raining,' she said. So what do you think Click did? He went outside and climbed up on the roof of the Train-House . . .

... and he poured water out of a watering-can down the windows – pitter-patter! 'It's raining,' said Josie. 'Put on your mac, Bun!'

So Bun was able to wear his new mackintosh at last, and didn't everyone think he looked grand in it!

Once Josie had a very bad cold. She really *had* to go to bed. Bun and Click were very worried about her.

'We must get the doctor,' said Bun. So Click went to get him. He was a wise old brownie with spectacles and a long beard.

He felt Josie's hot little hand, and shook his head. 'You are very ill,' he said. 'I think you ought to go away to hospital and be nursed properly.'

'No, don't take darling Josie away!' begged Bun. '*We* will look after her. We will, we will! Don't take her away.'

'Josie really wants a good nurse,' said the doctor. 'That is why I think she should go. Well – I'll call in tonight and see if she is fit to go with me to hospital.'

Now that day Bun was very busy. He rushed round to Mrs. Trot-About and borrowed an apron and a cap.

Bun Dresses Up!

He and Click cooked some fish for Josie and made a most beautiful creamy milk-pudding. Then Bun dressed up . . .

. . . and when the doctor came, there was Bun in cap and apron looking just like a nurse, taking a tray of well-cooked food to Josie.

'Dear me!' said the doctor. 'So you have got a nurse after all – and she knows what food to give an ill person, too . . .'

'Well, in that case, I think you would be better at home and I don't think I will take you to hospital.'

Bun Makes A Good Nurse!

The doctor went, and Josie smiled at Bun. 'Thank you, Bun,' she said. 'You knew I didn't want to leave you. You *do* look nice!'

Bun nursed Josie very well indeed. He always wore his cap and apron when the doctor came. It did make Click laugh!

When Josie was better, Bun and Click gave a little party.
They asked Mrs. Trot-About, Mister Pop, the Old Woman
– and the doctor.

'Dear me!' said the doctor, as he sat down to a marvellous
tea. 'You do remind me of somebody, Bun. Now who
can it be?'

Bun laughed. He ran into the bedroom and put on his cap and apron. 'I remind you of Josie's nurse,' he said.

'Well, what a trick to play on a doctor!' said the brownie doctor. 'You *were* a good nurse. Here's good health to you, Josie!' And they all drank ginger-pop with a laugh!

Click was always losing his handkerchiefs, and Josie was cross with him. 'I shall tie your tail round your hanky,' she said.

So she did, and Click was rather miserable about it. He said that all the field-mice ran after him and teased him.

Bun Has A Good Idea!

So then Josie tied his hanky round his neck like a scarf, but when he wanted to sneeze he couldn't get it undone in time!

Then Bun had a good idea. 'Stuff it into his keyhole,' he said, 'and let Click wear his key round his neck.' So they did, and after that Click always had his hanky with him!

One day there was great excitement in the Train-House.
The Queen of Fairyland was coming that way. 'I shall
put up clean curtains,' said Josie.

'I will clean all the carriage windows,' said Bun. 'I will
polish the door-handle and make it bright,' said Click.

The Train-House Looks Lovely

So they were all busy, and made the little Train-House as smart as can be. 'Let's get some flags and hang them all round the house,' said Bun.

So they did – and dear me, it did look fine. Don't you think the Train-House looks lovely and gay with all its fluttering flags?

'When does the Queen come?' asked Click. 'About four o'clock,' said Josie. 'I will put a nice new bow round your neck.'

Bun had a collar as well as a bow. He felt rather grand. Josie put on a new pink dress with little bows all down the front.

'Now we'll go and stand by the door and watch,' she
said. 'We must shout "Hip-hurray!" and wave our hands.
Come along.'

'Here she comes! Here comes the Queen!' cried Bun.
And, sure enough, there was the lovely little golden
carriage, drawn by four snow-white rabbits.

The Queen saw the little Train-House, with its fluttering flags. 'Oh, what a dear little house!' she cried.

'Stop, rabbits! I want to visit it. How do you do, Josie, Click, and Bun? May I see your house?'

The Queen Stays To Tea!

Well, what do you think of that? 'Your Majesty, the kettle is boiling, will you have a cup of tea?' said Josie.

And the Queen sat down and had tea with Josie, Click and Bun. I really think it was the happiest day of their lives!

Once Josie sent Click out to do the shopping. She gave him a purse of money and a basket.

Click went to the butcher's and the grocer's, and soon his basket was very full. He felt rather important.

Click Can't Count!

When he went back home again, he gave Josie the basket and the change. 'But you haven't brought back enough money,' said Josie.

'Well, you see, I don't know how many pennies make a shilling,' said Click, and he burst into tears.

Josie told Bun that Click didn't know how many pennies made a shilling. 'Don't you think he ought to go to school?' she said.

'Of course,' said Bun. 'We will go to Mr. Rap in Toy Town, and see if he has room for Click.' So off they went.

Click Is Going To School!

Mr. Rap was a schoolmaster doll. He had a cane, but he had a nice smile, too. He said he had room for Click.

So Josie and Bun went home and told Click he was to go to school. He was so pleased. 'Can I have a pencil-box?' he said.

Josie bought Click a pencil-box. Bun bought him a satchel. He felt very grand.

The next morning he went off to school, with his satchel over his back. 'Goodbye!' he said. 'Be good!' called Josie.

Click Is Afraid!

But suddenly Click felt afraid of school. He didn't want to go. He thought Mr. Rap might give him the cane.

So he ran all the way back home again, and Josie and Bun were very cross with him. '*I* shall give you the cane if you do this,' said Josie.

Well, Click went off to school the next day, and this time
Josie went with him. He said good morning politely to
Mr. Rap.

'There's your seat, next to Micky Mole,' said Mr. Rap.
'Work hard, obey orders, and you'll do well.'

Click was given a slate and told to write his letters on it. But he drew Mr. Rap instead!

'Dear, dear!' said Mr. Rap. 'Did you think this was a drawing lesson? Well, you will have to do your writing when the others do their drawing. What a pity!'

Click soon settled down at school, and he began to learn his lessons very well. He could soon write his name on the blackboard.

But one day he came home crying. 'Micky Mole has nibbled off half my whiskers!' he said. 'I do look queer.'

Micky Mole Gets The Cane!

'I shall complain to Mr. Rap,' said Bun, very fiercely. So off he went. Mr. Rap sent for Micky Mole.

'I will *not* have my pupils nibbling each other's whiskers,' he said, and he gave poor Micky Mole the cane!

Click looked very funny with whiskers on only one side of his face. 'I'll see if I can buy you some more,' said Josie.

So she went shopping for whiskers, but all the shops said the same thing. 'Sorry Madam, we have no whiskers today.'

Sammy Squirrel Helps Josie!

Then Josie met Sammy Squirrel and told him all about Click's trouble. He pulled five red hairs from his fur.

'There you are!' he said. 'Put a dob of glue on the end, stick them on Click's cheek, and he will look grand!'

So Josie put glue on the ends of the hairs, and then she and Bun stuck them on Click's soft cheek. They looked fine!

'The only thing is – they are longer than the whiskers on Click's other cheek, and they are red, not black,' said Josie.

But Bun snipped them the right size. 'It doesn't matter about them being red,' he said. 'It's most unusual to have red *and* black whiskers.'

Micky Mole said he was sorry to Click, and gave him a bag of sweets. Click forgave him and shared the sweets with everyone else.

One day when Click got home from school there was no one in the Train-House. 'Josie!' he called. 'Bun! Where are you?'

Bun had been out shopping. He soon came back. He was surprised not to see Josie there.

Where Is Josie?

'What's keeping her?' he said. 'Well, Click, I had better get you your dinner, or you will be late for afternoon school.'

Josie still hadn't come back when they had finished their dinner. They went outside, but she was not coming. Where could she be?

Josie had gone to see her Aunt Josephine. On the way back she crossed a field, and did not see a little girl there.

But the little girl saw Josie and gave a cry of surprise. 'A live doll! Oh, how lovely! Come here, doll!'

Josie ran away, but the little girl ran after her – and, oh dear, she caught Josie and wouldn't let her go.

'You shall come home and live with me and my toys in my nursery,' said the little girl, and carried her away.

Poor Josie! She tried to get away, she struggled and cried, but it was no use. The little girl took her home.

She put her into the nursery. There were lots of other toys there. They stared in surprise at Josie.

When the little girl had gone out of the room, Josie spoke to the toys. 'Tell me how to escape, quick!'

'The door is shut and the window is closed,' said the teddy bear. 'You can't escape,' said the sailor doll.

Well, at home Bun and Click grew more and more worried about Josie. Click wouldn't go to school. 'I want Josie,' he said.

Bun went out and asked everyone if they had seen Josie. 'No,' said Bron the brownie. 'No,' said Pickles the pixie. 'No,' said Nobby the gnome.

Bun And Click Are Miserable!

When night came there was still no Josie. Bun put Click to bed. 'I want Josie,' said Click. 'Where's Josie, Bun?'

Bun went to bed too – but he was so miserable in the middle of the night that he got into Click's bed and they cuddled up and cried together.

The next day Josie begged the little girl to let her go. 'I have a bunny and a mouse to look after,' she said. 'Let me go, please.'

'No,' said the little girl. 'I am having a party this afternoon and I want to show you off to my friends. They *will* be surprised.'

The Sailor Doll Helps Josie!

Josie was so unhappy that all the toys felt sorry for her.
The sailor doll put his arm round her. 'I will help you,'
he said.

So what do you think he did? He climbed up to the bell,
and rang it! 'Now,' said he, 'when someone comes, run
out of the door, quickly!'

Josie, Click and Bun Again

Mary the maid came to see who was ringing the bell. She opened the door – and at once Josie ran out! How she ran!

She ran down the passage and out of the garden door. The dog saw her and chased her. The little girl ran after her, too.

Josie tore down the garden. She squeezed through the hedge. The dog was almost on top of her when she saw a rabbit-hole.

Down she went, and the dog couldn't follow her! Josie ran right down and down – and came to a most surprised rabbit-family.

'What's the matter?' cried the father rabbit. Josie told him.
He was very glad she had escaped. 'Now you sit down
for a rest,' he said.

Then he took Josie home, because she didn't know the
way. He was so nice to her. He said his name was Woffly.

Josie Comes Home!

Click and Bun were just going to go to the police-station
to tell the policeman to look for Josie, when . . .

. . . They suddenly saw her coming with Woffly! 'Josie
darling!' cried Bun, and hugged her. 'Oh, Josie, Josie!'
said Click, and tears of joy ran down his whiskers.

Josie told Click and Bun how kind the sailor doll and Woffly, the rabbit, had been to her. 'I shall knit them each a jumper,' she said.

So she knitted a red one for the rabbit and a blue one for the sailor doll.

She asked them to come to tea, and *how* pleased they were with their new jumpers. Woffly looked lovely in his.

While Josie washed up the tea-things, Woffly chatted with Bun and the sailor doll taught Click to dance the hornpipe. You *should* have seen him dance it!

When the end of term came, Josie heard that there was to be a concert and a prize-giving. Click gave her the invitation.

'I shan't get a prize,' he said. 'I still don't know how many pennies make a shilling. But I did try hard, Josie.'

A Lovely Concert!

'Well, we will all go to your concert and hear you sing,'
said Josie. So, when the day came, they all set off.

They sat down in their seats and watched the children of
Mr. Rap's school singing and reciting. They were very
good.

Josie and Bun had a great surprise when Click came on to dance all by himself. He wore a sailor's cap.

He danced the hornpipe dance just as the sailor doll had taught him. How everyone clapped!

Click Wins A Prize!

And would you believe it, Click got the prize for dancing!
'You still don't know how many pennies there are in a
shilling, but you dance very well,' said Mr. Rap.

So they all went home happily, and Click carried his prize
book himself all the way, though it was nearly as big as
he was!

Click was so proud of his prize that he took it to show a family of dormice he knew.

'It's a nice prize,' they said, 'but we think you are a baby, Click, because you don't know how many pennies there are in a shilling.'

Click Breaks A Shilling!

Then Click was angry. 'I will really find out,' he said, and he took a hammer. He put a shilling down on the ground.

And he hammered the shilling into little bits. But, oh dear, he couldn't find any pennies in it at all!

Then Click did his sailor dance to show the dormice. He did it on a high branch so that they could see him.

But oh, he fell off, and got caught in an enormous spider's web below. The spider came out . . .

'Don't have me for your dinner, please don't,' begged
Click. 'Help, help! Josie! Bun!'

'I'll teach you to spoil my web!' said the spider, angrily.
'I'll roll you up in my thread till you can't move!'

So when Josie and Bun came to find Click, all they found
was a funny little cocoon-like thing . . .

. . . that rolled about and squeaked. 'Why, it's poor Click!'
said Josie. 'Quick, undo him, Bun!'

Happy Ending!

They undid him and took him home to have a bath. He was sad and cried on Josie's shoulder.

But how he cheered up when Josie read him his prize. What *do* you think it was? Why, it was '*Josie, Click and Bun Again.*' Wasn't that a lovely surprise!

Join the RED FOX Reader's Club

The Red Fox Reader's Club is for readers of all ages. All you have to do is ask your local bookseller or librarian for a Red Fox Reader's Club card. As an official Red Fox Reader you only have to borrow or buy eight Red Fox books in order to qualify for your own Red Fox Reader's Clubpack – full of exciting surprises! If you have any difficulty obtaining a Red Fox Reader's Club card please write to: Random House Children's Books Marketing Department, 20 Vauxhall Bridge Road, London SW1V 2SA.